I Will Always Love You

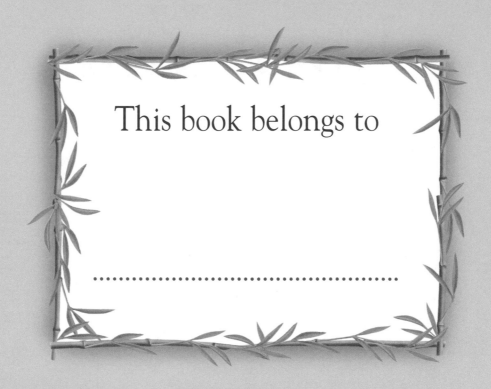

This book belongs to

....

ISBN 0-439-60722-1

12 11 10 9 8 7 6   7 8/0

Printed in the U.S.A.   08

First Scholastic printing, October 2003

I Will Always Love You

illustrated by Trace Moroney
written by Jane E. Gerver

SCHOLASTIC INC.
New York Toronto London Auckland Sydney
Mexico City New Delhi Hong Kong Buenos Aires

Little Panda hid in a tree. His mother was busy gathering bamboo for supper. And Little Panda was supposed to be helping her.

"Where are you, Little Panda?" called Mother.

"Bam-BOO!" Little Panda shouted, jumping out from behind the tree.

"Oh, you startled me!" said Mother. "You are not being a help at all."

"Do you still love me?" asked Little Panda.
"Of course," said his mother. "I will *always* love you!"

"But what if I did something very naughty?" asked
Little Panda. "What if I went off to climb the highest

mountain in the world, where it was cold and snowy, and I didn't take my jacket?"

"Not taking a jacket on a long and chilly adventure *would* be a little bit naughty," Mother said.

"But I would still love you," she added with a smile.

With a sigh, Little Panda slipped his paw into his
mother's larger one and leaned into her.

"But what if I took my jacket and went off to sail
the seven seas—without leaving you a note?" he asked.

"Not letting me know where you had gone *would* be a little bit naughty," said Mother.

"But I would still love you," she added, giving his little paw a loving squeeze.

"What if I left you a note telling you I was off
fighting a big dragon and saving the whole world.

But I didn't wear my rain boots and I got my
feet wet?" asked Little Panda.

"Not wearing boots during a rainstorm—especially with a dragon nearby—*would* be a little bit naughty," said Mother.

"But I would still love you even then," she added, giving
her little panda a big, fuzzy hug.

"What if I wore my jacket and my boots and
left you a note that I was flying around the world—

but I forgot to come home in time for
supper?" asked Little Panda.

"It would be wonderful to see the whole wide world,
but not coming home in time for supper *would* be a little

bit naughty," said Mother. "Even so, I would still love
you," she added, giving her little panda a soft, furry kiss.

"What if I came home in time for supper, but I took all
the bamboo we were going to eat?" asked Little Panda.

"Why? What would you do with it?" asked Mother
in surprise.

"I'll show you," said Little Panda. He took Mother by the hand and led her around the tree.

"See?" said Little Panda. "I will always love you, too!"